Authors' Note

"She'll Be Comin' Round the Mountain," originally a black spiritual called "When the Chariot Comes," became a popular Appalachian song during the 1800s. It was also sung by railroad workers as they laid tracks across America in the late nineteenth century.

Our version of the song began when a playmate of our oldest daughter's came to visit us in our new home. Despite fears that time and distance might have eroded their friendship, they found—to their delight—it still to be very much intact. During the week of the visit, hiking and driving in the car, we sang "She'll Be Comin' Round the Mountain" many times. Since the song never tells you the name of the person who's coming around the mountain, we began to speculate about who "she" might be. What follows in this book are the results of that speculation.

Happy reading . . . and singing.

—Tom Birdseye and Debbie Holsclaw Birdseye

For Travis, and all of our friends, both silver and gold
T.B. and D.H.B.
For Kate, who loves the mountains
A.G.

Text copyright © 1994 by Tom Birdseye and Debbie Holsclaw Birdseye
Illustrations copyright © 1994 by Andrew Glass
All rights reserved
Printed in the United States of America
First Edition
Library of Congress Cataloging-in-Publication Data
Birdseye, Tom.
She'll be comin' round the mountain / by Tom and Debbie Birdseye ;
illustrated by Andrew Glass.
p.   cm.
Summary: Family members compose verses to the folk song "She'll Be
Coming 'Round the Mountain" to describe an expected visitor.
ISBN 0-8234-1032-3
[1. Singing—Fiction.   2. Friendship—Fiction.   3. Mountain life—
Fiction.]   I. Birdseye, Debbie.   II. Glass, Andrew, ill.
III. Title.   IV. Title: She'll be coming around the mountain.
PZ7.B5213Sh   1994   92-37641   CIP   AC
[E]—dc20

She'll Be Comin' Round the Mountain

adapted by Tom Birdseye
and Debbie Holsclaw Birdseye

illustrated by Andrew Glass

Holiday House/New York

Oma and Opa Sweet and all the clan sat on the front porch wearing smiles a mile wide. It'd been years since they'd last seen their dear friend, Tootie. But now a letter had arrived announcing that she'd be comin' round the mountain for a visit. Tootie! After all this time! Goodness gracious! Lorda' mercy! Yahoo!

"Yahoo!" That had always been the first thing Tootie said when she used to drop by. Then she'd dance a little jig right there in the front yard. "Yahoo!" Now it made Opa and Oma Sweet and all the clan grin like Christmas just remembering it.

But the twins, Petunia and Delbert, had never met dear Tootie. They hadn't been born when she'd last visited. "When will she get here?" they kept wanting to know. "When, Oma? When?"

Opa Sweet smiled, then looked at Oma Sweet
and commenced to humming. Oma Sweet nodded, then
started tapping her foot in time.
She began to sing.

She'll be comin' round the mountain
   when she comes. (Yes, indeed!)
She'll be comin' round the mountain
   when she comes. (Yes, indeed!)
She'll be comin' round the mountain,
she'll be comin' round the mountain,
She'll be comin' round the mountain
   when she comes. (Yes, indeed!)

"Will Tootie come by train?" asked Petunia. She had always wanted to go meet the train.

Papa Sweet picked up his old guitar and strummed a chord. "Naw," he said, "not Tootie."

She'll drive her old jalopy when she comes. (Beep! Beep!)
She'll drive her old jalopy when she comes. (Beep! Beep!)
She'll drive her old jalopy, she'll drive her old jalopy,
She'll drive her old jalopy when she comes. (Beep! Beep!)

"Yeah, but there're lots of old jalopies around here," said little Delbert. "How will we know it's her?"

Mama Sweet gave little Delbert a hug, then plucked her banjo. "Know it's Tootie?" she said. "Nary a problem there."

She'll be wearing jeans and slop boots when she comes.
    (Mighty fine!)
She'll be wearing jeans and slop boots when she comes.
    (Mighty fine!)
She'll be wearing jeans and slop boots, she'll be wearing jeans
    and slop boots,
She'll be wearing jeans and slop boots when she comes.
    (Mighty fine!)

Petunia and Delbert both giggled. "Tell us more about Tootie!" they begged. "Pleeease!"

Aunt Ophelia ran the bow across her fiddle, sending notes flying high.

She'll bring her old pig Clovis when she comes. (Oink! Oink!)
She'll bring her old pig Clovis when she comes. (Oink! Oink!)
She'll bring her old pig Clovis, she'll bring her old pig Clovis,
She'll bring her old pig Clovis when she comes. (Oink! Oink!)

"A pig named Clovis?" laughed Petunia.
"Riding in Tootie's car?" giggled Delbert.

"Yessireebob," Uncle Burgoo drawled, hauling his big bass fiddle out of the corner, then thumping out a deep bottom line. "But that's not all!"

She'll bring all of her farm critters when she comes. (Look a' there!)
She'll bring all of her farm critters when she comes. (Look a' there!)
She'll bring all of her farm critters, she'll bring all of her farm critters,
She'll bring all of her farm critters when she comes. (Look a' there!)

"Yahoo!" yelled little Delbert and Petunia. "Yay, Tootie!"

Cousin Putney joined in, playing the washboard in rhythm with the tune. Cousin Sol clacked the spoons. Everyone sang—high, low, and in the middle. "Sweet harmony," those on the porch called it.

She'll twirl and swing and curtsy when she comes. (Swish! Swish!)
She'll twirl and swing and curtsy when she comes. (Swish! Swish!)
She'll twirl and swing and curtsy, she'll twirl and swing and curtsy,
She'll twirl and swing and curtsy when she comes. (Swish! Swish!)

Just then a big cloud of dust
appeared round the mountain. "It's
Tootie!" Oma and Opa Sweet and
all the clan sang. Aunt Annie started
clog dancing, stomping her heels
and clicking her toes. Then
everybody joined in.

Oh, we'll all dance out to meet her when she comes. (Promenade!)
Oh, we'll all dance out to meet her when she comes. (Promenade!)
Oh, we'll all dance out to meet her, we'll all dance out to meet her,
Oh, we'll all dance out to meet her when she comes. (Promenade!)

The cloud of dust rolled closer.

"Yahoo! Yahoo!" yelled Oma and Opa Sweet and all the clan as they do-si-doed across the yard.

The cloud of dust rolled to a stop.
"She'll be comin' round the mountain!" everyone sang.
But when the cloud of dust cleared . . .

"Tootie?" said Oma and Opa Sweet and all the clan. "Is that *you*?" Because all of a sudden they weren't sure. It had been so long, and she'd been so far away.

The fine lady turned this way and that, pulling her silk gloves off one finger at a time.

"Tootie?" Would she still be their friend? "*Tootie?*" Oh my!

The fine lady smiled and batted her long, fancy eyelashes.

Then she threw back her head and yelled:

"TOOTIE!!" Oma and Opa Sweet and all the clan cried. Time and change didn't matter. She was *still* their dear friend Tootie.

"Yahoo!" said Tootie again, and danced a little jig. Oma and Opa Sweet and all the clan couldn't help but join in.

Oh, we'll sing, friends all together, when she comes. *(YAHOO!)*
Oh, we'll sing, friends all together, when she comes. *(YAHOO!)*
Oh, we'll sing, friends all together, we'll sing, friends all together,
Oh, we'll sing, friends all together, when she comes. *(YAHOO!*
    YAHOO! YAHOOOOOOOO!)

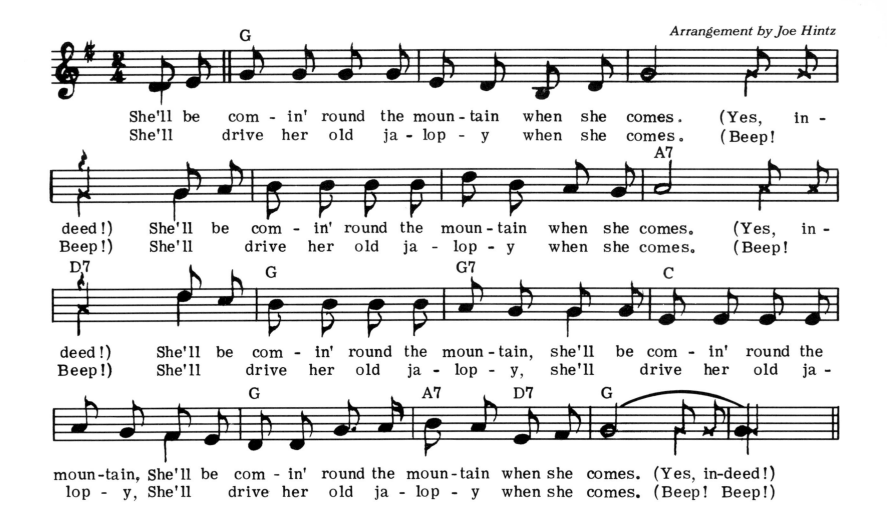

Arrangement by Joe Hintz

She'll be com - in' round the moun - tain when she comes. (Yes, in -
She'll drive her old ja - lop - y when she comes. (Beep!

deed!) She'll be com - in' round the moun - tain when she comes. (Yes, in -
Beep!) She'll drive her old ja - lop - y when she comes. (Beep!

deed!) She'll be com - in' round the moun - tain, she'll be com - in' round the
Beep!) She'll drive her old ja - lop - y, she'll drive her old ja -

moun - tain, She'll be com - in' round the moun - tain when she comes. (Yes, in-deed!)
lop - y, She'll drive her old ja - lop - y when she comes. (Beep! Beep!)

She'll be wearing jeans and slop boots when she comes. (Mighty fine!)
She'll be wearing jeans and slop boots when she comes. (Mighty fine!)
She'll be wearing jeans and slop boots, she'll be wearing jeans and slop boots,
She'll be wearing jeans and slop boots when she comes. (Mighty fine!)

She'll bring her old pig Clovis when she comes. (Oink! Oink!)
She'll bring her old pig Clovis when she comes. (Oink! Oink!)
She'll bring her old pig Clovis, she'll bring her old pig Clovis,
She'll bring her old pig Clovis when she comes. (Oink! Oink!)

She'll bring all of her farm critters when she comes. (Look a' there!)
She'll bring all of her farm critters when she comes. (Look a' there!)
She'll bring all of her farm critters, she'll bring all of her farm critters,
She'll bring all of her farm critters when she comes. (Look a' there!)

She'll twirl and swing and curtsy when she comes. (Swish! Swish!)
She'll twirl and swing and curtsy when she comes. (Swish! Swish!)
She'll twirl and swing and curtsy, she'll twirl and swing and curtsy,
She'll twirl and swing and curtsy when she comes. (Swish! Swish!)

Oh, we'll all dance out to meet her when she comes. (Promenade!)
Oh, we'll all dance out to meet her when she comes. (Promenade!)
Oh, we'll all dance out to meet her, we'll all dance out to meet her,
Oh, we'll all dance out to meet her when she comes. (Promenade!)

Oh, we'll sing, friends all together, when she comes. (YAHOO!)
Oh, we'll sing, friends all together, when she comes. (YAHOO!)
Oh, we'll sing, friends all together, we'll sing, friends all together,
Oh, we'll sing, friends all together, when she comes. (YAHOO! YAHOO!
YAHOOOOOOOO!